Gotcha! Gotcha Back!

by Nancy Krulik • illustrated by John & Wendy

Grosset & Dunlap

To Danielle, Scott, and Talia, and
all the children at the Heschel School—NK
For John L. Walters: inventor of the
tongue-in-cheek extractor—J&W

GROSSET & DUNLAP
Published by the Penguin Group
Penguin Group (USA) Inc., 375 Hudson Street,
New York, New York 10014, U.S.A.
Penguin Group (Canada), 90 Eglinton Avenue East, Suite 700,
Toronto, Ontario, Canada M4P 2Y3
(a division of Pearson Penguin Canada Inc.)
Penguin Books Ltd, 80 Strand, London WC2R 0RL, England
Penguin Ireland, 25 St Stephen's Green, Dublin 2, Ireland
(a division of Penguin Books Ltd)
Penguin Group (Australia), 250 Camberwell Road,
Camberwell, Victoria 3124, Australia
(a division of Pearson Australia Group Pty Ltd)
Penguin Books India Pvt Ltd, 11 Community Centre,
Panchsheel Park, New Delhi - 110 017, India
Penguin Group (NZ), Cnr Airborne and Rosedale Roads,
Albany, Auckland 1310, New Zealand
(a division of Pearson New Zealand Ltd)
Penguin Books (South Africa) (Pty) Ltd, 24 Sturdee Avenue,
Rosebank, Johannesburg 2196, South Africa

Penguin Books Ltd, Registered Offices:
80 Strand, London WC2R 0RL, England

Text copyright © 2006 by Nancy Krulik. Illustrations copyright © 2006 by
John and Wendy. All rights reserved. Published by Grosset & Dunlap, a
division of Penguin Young Readers Group, 345 Hudson Street, New York,
New York 10014. GROSSET & DUNLAP is a trademark of Penguin Group
(USA) Inc. Printed in the U.S.A.

Library of Congress Control Number: 2005019196

ISBN 0-448-43768-6   10 9 8

Chapter 1

Dear Katie,
This is a picture of the rain forest here in Peru. Today I saw a magnificent macaw bird and watched monkeys swinging in the trees! Tomorrow I am going on an Amazon River cruise. I'll have a lot of pictures to show you when I get home.
Love,
Grandma

Katie Carew
32 Cherrydale Lane
Cherrydale U.S.A.

Katie Carew stared at the brightly colored postcard in her hands. "Lucky Grandma!" she told her brown and white cocker spaniel, Pepper. "I'd love to see a monkey in the wild. The only ones I've seen have been in zoos."

Pepper wagged his tail, and then ran off to play with his pal, Snowball, the white puppy who lived next door.

Katie knew all about how much fun vacations could be. She and her parents had spent their last vacation in Europe. They had gone to England, France, Spain, and Italy. Katie had met artists, dancers, gondoliers, and a very funny palace guard. It had all been so exciting.

But that was then. This was *now*. And now wasn't very exciting at all.

Katie took the rest of the mail from the mailbox and started to walk back toward her house. She looked around. Her front yard wasn't nearly as pretty as the picture of the jungle on her grandmother's postcard. There was only one tree on Katie's lawn, and there were no monkeys or macaws in its branches.

In fact, the only animals in sight were Pepper and Snowball. They were busy chasing their tails.

Dogs certainly weren't as interesting as monkeys and macaws.

Just then, Katie's good friend George Brennan came riding by on his skateboard.

"Hey, Katie Kazoo, what's new?" he asked Katie, using the way-cool nickname he had given her.

"Nothing," Katie answered. "Everything's just the same."

"Tell me about it," George said. "This town is so boring." He reached into his back pocket and pulled out a slim newspaper. "Did you see this week's copy of the *Class 4A Express*?"

"I forgot to take one when I left school today," Katie answered.

"That's okay, you can have mine," George told her, handing over the paper.

" 'Beginning Band Plays "Mary Had a Little Lamb" in School Concert,' " Katie read one of the headlines. " 'Fourth Grade Plays Volleyball,' " she added, reading another.

"Can you believe that's the big news in our class?" George asked. "I sure wish things could be more interesting around here."

Katie gulped. George had just made a wish. That was not a good thing at all.

Wishes were dangerous.

Katie learned all about them on one really bad day back in third grade. That day she had dropped the ball and lost a football game for her team. Then she'd gotten mud all over her favorite pants. Worst of all, she'd let out a giant burp in front of the whole class. That had been *so* embarrassing!

That night, Katie had wished that she could be anyone but herself. There must have been a shooting star flying overhead, because the next day the magic wind came.

The magic wind was a big tornado that

swirled only around Katie. It was so powerful that it could turn her into somebody else!

The first time the magic wind came, it turned Katie into Speedy, the class 3A hamster. She'd escaped from her cage and wound up inside George's stinky sneaker. YUCK!

Since then the magic wind had been back again and again. One time it turned her into Mr. Starkey, the school music teacher. The band sounded really terrible when Katie was the conductor!

Another time the magic wind switcherooed Katie into their school principal, Mr. Kane. By the end of the day, the cafeteria was covered in paint, kids were running wild in the halls, and all the electricity had gone out in the school.

The worst thing about the magic wind was that every time it came, the person Katie turned into got in big trouble. Then it was up to Katie to make things all right again. That wasn't always so easy.

Katie didn't make wishes anymore. They

caused too many problems. She figured George probably shouldn't be making any wishes either.

"Forget about it, George," Katie told her friend. "Things in Cherrydale will always be the same. I should know. I have lived here all my life."

George shook his head. "Things can change, Katie," he told her. "Life in Cherrydale could get really interesting—with a little help from us."

Katie looked at him curiously. What was George talking about?

"Why don't you ride your bike over to my house?" George suggested. "I'll show you!"

"Sure," Katie agreed. "Let me just tell my mom where I'm going." Katie couldn't wait to find out what George had in mind.

Chapter 2

"Okay, check this out!" George exclaimed proudly as he and Katie sat on his back porch. He held up a big cardboard box. "My cousin Charlie sent this to me for my birthday."

Katie watched as George reached into the box and pulled out a big, gray, hairy spider! "How did this get in here?" George shouted out. Quickly, he threw the spider across the porch.

It landed right on Katie's lap! "AAAAHH!" Katie screamed.

George began to laugh. "Relax, Katie Kazoo. It's just a fake spider." He laughed even harder.

"You scared me, George," Katie said angrily.

"Oh, come on. It's just a joke," George told her. "Look what else my cousin got me."

Katie peered inside the box. There was a clear plastic cube with a fly inside it, a pencil, a camera, and two packs of gum. *What a weird group of gifts*, she thought.

"Can I have a piece of the gum?" Katie asked George.

"Sure." George smiled slightly as he handed Katie a stick of gum.

Katie unwrapped the gum and popped it in her mouth. A minute later she spit it right out. "Blech!" Katie exclaimed. "That tastes like dirt."

"You should see your face!" George exclaimed, laughing. "I've got to get a picture of you." He pulled his camera out of the box, pointed it toward Katie and . . .

"Oh!" Katie shouted angrily. She looked down at her shirt. It was all wet.

"Gotcha!" George exclaimed. "It's a water-gun camera!"

Katie shook her head. "That's not funny," she said.

"Sure it is," George said, laughing. "But not as funny as this gum that stains your teeth black." He picked up the other pack of gum. "Imagine how freaked out Miriam Chan would be if you gave her a piece of this!"

Katie frowned. "That would be mean, George," she told him.

"Nah," George disagreed. "It would be funny. And we need a few laughs at our school."

Katie shook her head. She wasn't so sure that practical jokes were a good way to make things *un*-boring.

"I don't want to play jokes on people, George," Katie told him.

"You don't have to," George said. "*I* will." He stopped and thought for a moment. "Hey, didn't you get a whoopee cushion and fake throw-up from your Secret Santa last Christmas?"

Katie sighed, remembering how disappointed she had been when she had opened those gifts. They weren't the kinds of things she liked at all.

But they sure were the kinds of things George liked. Fake throw-up and a whoopee cushion would have been the perfect presents for him.

"Tell you what, Katie Kazoo," George

continued. "I'll trade you a rubber pencil for them." He held up the wiggly yellow pencil. "Next time Kadeem asks to borrow a pencil from you, you can give him this one. It doesn't write!"

Katie thought about that. It *was* kind of annoying the way Kadeem Carter always seemed to have to borrow her pencils. Especially because he chewed them up before giving them back.

"I guess that would serve him right," she said slowly.

"Sure it would," George agreed. "So what do you say? We could start tomorrow. We'll call it Funny Friday!"

"Okay," Katie said, taking the pencil from George. "I'll bring the whoopee cushion and the plastic throw-up to school tomorrow. Just promise not to be too mean, okay?"

"I promise," George assured her.

Chapter 3

"Do you want to write an article for this week's *4A Express*?" Mandy Banks asked Katie on Friday morning as they walked into their classroom.

Katie shook her head. "Not this week. I don't have any ideas for an article."

Mandy frowned. "That's the problem. Nobody does. How am I supposed to edit a newspaper when no one wants to write for it?"

Katie felt bad for Mandy. She remembered when Jeremy Fox, one of her two best friends, had been the editor of their third-grade newspaper, the *3A Times*. It had been a huge job. Jeremy had spent a lot of time writing articles on his computer.

Being editor of a class newspaper was a big responsibility. Mandy really could use some help from the rest of the class.

Still, it wasn't really the other kids' fault that there wasn't much to write about. "There really hasn't been a whole lot of news here at school lately," Katie reminded Mandy.

"AAAAHHHHHHH!"

Before Mandy could answer her, somebody screamed. Everybody turned around to see Emma Stavros standing on top of her beanbag chair, pointing toward the floor.

Mr. Guthrie raced over to Emma S. The kids ran over, too.

"What's wrong?" Mr. G. asked Emma S.

Emma S. gulped. "It's a M-m-mouse!" she stammered nervously.

Katie looked down at the floor. Sure enough, there was a little gray mouse on the ground next to Emma S.'s beanbag chair.

Katie stared at the furry little creature

for a minute. There was something strange about it. "It's not moving," she told Emma S. "Usually mice are so afraid of people, they run away as soon as they see them."

"Maybe it's a *dead* mouse," Kevin Camilleri suggested.

"AAAAAAHHHHHHH!" Emma S. shouted even louder this time.

"I don't think so," Mr. G. told Kevin. The teacher reached down and picked up the ball of gray fluff.

"Ooh, gross!" Emma S. gasped.

"Relax, Emma," Mr. G. told her. "This mouse isn't real. Someone was playing a joke on you."

Emma S. opened her eyes wide. She looked like she was going to cry.

"Whose mouse is this?" Mr. Guthrie asked.

Nobody answered.

"Come on, dudes, 'fess up," Mr. G. urged.

Still no one answered.

"Okay," Mr. G. said finally. "Well, whoever you are, I hope you learned that practical jokes like this aren't always funny."

Katie was pretty sure she knew who had planted the fake mouse in the classroom. George's Funny Friday had begun.

Of course Katie would never tell on George. Only a rat told on her friends. And Katie wasn't a rat.

Katie looked over to see if George was laughing. But he had his face turned away. He was pretending to look into Slinky's cage.

"Slinky sure looks disappointed," George said as he stared at the class snake. "He sure would have liked to eat a mouse."

"Well, *I'm* not disappointed that the mouse is fake," Emma S. said.

"Me either," Emma Weber agreed. "Whoever put that mouse there was really mean. It's not nice to scare someone like that."

"Man, Emma S., you really freaked out!" Kevin said with a chuckle.

"That was the loudest scream I ever heard," Kadeem added. "I'll bet they heard you all the way in China."

Soon all the boys were laughing at how scared Emma S. had been of the fake mouse.

"Okay, dudes, let's settle down," Mr. G. urged the class. "It's time for social studies."

Kadeem leaned over toward Katie's

beanbag. "Can I borrow a pencil?" he asked
her.

Katie thought about the bendy rubber
pencil in her bookbag. But she couldn't give it
to him. It was just too mean.

"Sure," Katie said as she pulled a regular
pencil out of her bag.

"Thanks," Kadeem said. "I'll give it back to
you at the end of class," he added.

Katie watched as Kadeem placed the
pencil in his mouth and chewed on the eraser.

"Keep it," she told him with a sigh.

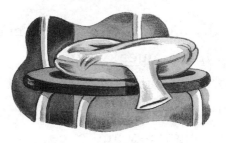

Chapter 4

"I have definitely learned how to walk like a model," Katie's best friend Suzanne Lock told a few of the fourth-graders as they waited in the lunch line that afternoon. "You have to keep your chin up. Like this."

Suzanne raised her head high and began walking over to one of the tables.

"You look like a real model," Jessica Haynes told Suzanne. "Is that hard to do?"

"It's *very* difficult," Suzanne told her. "I've been taking modeling classes for months to learn how to do it."

"It's not so hard," Kevin Camilleri argued. He raised his chin way up and began to wiggle his hips really hard. "Look at me. I'm a model," he said in a high, squeaky voice.

"Me too," Kadeem said. He sucked in his cheeks really hard and pretended to throw kisses to an imaginary audience.

"Boys!" Suzanne huffed as she began to sit down in one of the cafeteria chairs. "They don't know anything about modeling. It's really very hard. You have to be really graceful to—"

Before she could finish her sentence, a loud, gassy noise came from her rear end.

"Whoa!" Kadeem laughed.

"Check it out!" Andrew Epstein added. "The great model cut the cheese!"

Suzanne stood up right away. "I did not!" she shouted.

"Ooh, stinky!"

Manny Gonzalez said, moving his chair far away from Suzanne's.

"Who put this here?" Suzanne demanded. She picked up a pink rubber whoopee cushion that had been left on her seat.

Katie looked around. All the boys were laughing, but George was laughing the hardest.

Suzanne turned to George, and threw the whoopee cushion right at him. "I hate you, George Brennan!" she exclaimed.

"I don't know what you're talking about," George insisted. But the smile on his face proved he did.

"Who cares who did it? It was great!" Kevin chuckled. "Somebody really gotcha, Suzanne!"

"It *was* funny," Jeremy Fox agreed. He turned to Suzanne. "You deserved it. You were being such a snob."

"Yeah, well, you're a *slob*!" Suzanne snapped back at him. She pointed to a big pizza-grease stain on Jeremy's shirt.

Katie frowned. Suzanne was her best friend. But so was Jeremy. It made her sad that they didn't like each other.

"Come on, Suzanne, chill out. It was just a joke," Manny told her.

Suzanne shook her head. "No way. Jokes are funny. That wasn't funny at all."

George shook his head. "Wanna bet?" he asked her. "Everybody here thought it was hysterical. That joke definitely livened things up in this cafeteria. Didn't it, Katie Kazoo?"

Katie turned away. She had to admit that it had been pretty funny. But she could never say that to Suzanne. Especially since it was Katie's whoopee cushion. Suzanne would be really angry at Katie if she found out about that.

"You can deny it, George, but I know you put that whoopee cushion there," Suzanne insisted. "And I'm going to get you back. Just you wait and see."

George laughed even harder. "Ooooh," he said as he pretended to shake and shiver. "I'm soooo scared!"

Chapter 5

Saturday was cold and rainy. But the kids in Katie's cooking club didn't mind. Saturday was the day they met at Katie's house to try out new recipes. They were all nice and dry inside, making chocolate-covered bananas.

"Mmmm," Becky Stern murmured as she took a bite of hers. "This is the yummiest!"

"I wish we'd made more," George grumbled. "Mine's all gone, and I'm still hungry."

"Me too," Jeremy agreed.

"You know what I feel like?" Kevin asked the others. "Pizza."

"Funny, you don't *look* like a pizza," George joked.

But everyone agreed that a pizza sure would taste good. And before long, Katie, George, Jeremy, Suzanne, Miriam, Jessica, Kevin, Mandy, and Becky were all at the Cherrydale Mall, watching as Louie threw pizza dough high in the air.

"When the moon, hits your eye, like a big pizza pie . . . " Louie sang as he tossed the dough. Luckily the pizza didn't hit Louie in the eye. He caught it with his hands instead.

"I really hate rain," Jeremy groaned. "This is the third weekend in a row that my afternoon soccer game has been rained out."

Becky wasn't sad. She was smiling. "I'm glad it rained. I hardly ever see you on the weekends," she told Jeremy.

Jeremy scowled.

Katie felt bad for Jeremy. Becky was always saying things like that to him. And Jeremy hated it when she did.

"All right!" George exclaimed happily. "Louie just put our pie in the oven. Half extra cheese and half mushroom!"

A few minutes later, Louie placed the steaming hot pizza on the table, and handed everyone a dish.

"Mmm . . . extra cheesy!" George exclaimed as he grabbed for a slice.

"Here, George," Suzanne said sweetly as she handed him the saltshaker. "I know how much you love salt on your pizza."

Katie didn't know how anyone could put salt on pizza. But George did. He loved salty foods.

"Gee, thanks, Suzanne," George replied. He took the saltshaker from her. He started to turn it over onto his pizza, but stopped suddenly. Then he shook his head. "Unfortunately, I don't like sugar on my pizza!"

"What?" Suzanne asked him.

"This saltshaker is filled with sugar," George said, putting a little on his finger and tasting it. "Nice try, Suzanne, but that's the oldest practical joke in the world. *I* would never fall for it."

Suzanne sighed. "You're pretty good, George."

George shook his head. "No I'm not," he disagreed. "I'm the best."

"Okay," Suzanne admitted. "You're the best. And you know what? I'm not even mad at you anymore." She held out her hand. "Let's be friends again."

"We're not friends," George told her. "Besides, you have a buzzer on your hand. And I'm not falling for that either."

Suzanne frowned. She'd been caught . . . again.

"Go, George!" Kevin exclaimed. "No one can pull a practical joke on you!"

George grinned and took a huge bite of his pizza.

"This cheese is getting all over my hands," Miriam Chan said. "I'm going to get some more napkins."

As Miriam walked over to the counter, Katie noticed George reaching across the table. But from where she was sitting she couldn't see exactly what he was doing.

A moment later, Miriam came back to the table. She put the napkins in the center and sat down. Then she started to take a sip of her drink . . .

"Oh, yuck!" she exclaimed. "There's a fly in my water!" Miriam jumped up to get away from the bug. As she stood, she hit the edge of the table. The water spilled all over her jeans.

Kevin and George started laughing.

"Check it out," Kevin exclaimed. "Miriam wet her pants!" He laughed even harder.

Mandy looked over at the ice and water that had spilled on the table. She picked up one of the cubes and examined it.

"This isn't an ice cube," she told Miriam. "It's a piece of clear plastic with a fake bug in it. Somebody put it in your water to scare you."

"And I know who," Suzanne said. She stared right at George.

"Who, me?" George asked. "I was just sitting here, eating my pizza." He gobbled down the last bite. "And I'm finished now. So I'm leaving."

"Me too," Kevin added. He stood up and followed behind his best friend.

"I know it was George who did that," Suzanne said as the boys left. "I'm sure of it.

"I wish we could get him back for his dumb practical jokes," Miriam said with a frown.

Mandy smiled. "Oh, I think we can," she said mysteriously.

Katie gulped. She didn't like the sound of that at all.

Chapter 6

"Can you believe Mr. Kane?" Suzanne exclaimed angrily as she and Katie stood on the school steps on Monday afternoon. "Why should we all have to miss recess just because George played another of his practical jokes on everyone?"

"Suzanne, you don't know for sure it was George," Katie said.

"Come on, Katie," Suzanne argued. "Who else would put a piece of plastic throw-up in the salad bar at school?"

Katie frowned. The fake throw-up was actually hers. She was just lucky Suzanne hadn't remembered that Katie had gotten it from her Secret Santa.

"Lots of people could have done it," Katie said. "Anyone could buy plastic throw-up at the toy store."

Suzanne shrugged. "I guess. But George is the only person in the world who would put it in the salad bar."

Katie couldn't argue with that. So she changed the subject instead. "You want to come over to my house and do homework?" she asked.

Suzanne shook her head. "Sorry. I have plans with Mandy today."

Katie looked at her strangely. Suzanne and Mandy hardly ever hung out together.

"Oh," she said slowly. "What are you guys doing?"

"Nothing special," Suzanne said with a shrug.

Katie waited for Suzanne to ask her if she wanted to come, too.

Suzanne didn't say a word.

Just then, Mandy came walking out of the school. "Hey, Suzanne. Hi, Katie."

"Hi," Katie replied.

"Are you ready?" Suzanne asked Mandy.

Mandy looked over at Katie. "Uh, sure," she murmured. "I just . . . um . . . er . . . I have to go back and get something out of my classroom first."

"Oh, okay," Suzanne said. "I'll come with you." She turned to Katie. "See you later," she added.

"Yeah, later," Katie answered as she watched the two girls head into the school building together.

There was something really suspicious about Suzanne and Mandy's behavior. Katie couldn't figure out what was going on, but she knew something was up.

There was only one way to find out what it was. Quickly, Katie hurried up the steps and back into the school.

Katie knew that it was wrong to spy on people. But she couldn't help herself. She had to know what the girls were up to. Quickly, she followed the girls down the hallway.

"Wait, do you hear somebody?" Mandy asked, suddenly stopping in her tracks.

Katie gasped, and then ducked down under a nearby water fountain.

"I don't see anyone," Suzanne said, looking around. "Come on, we have to hurry."

"We have to be careful, too," Mandy reminded her. "We don't want to get caught in the computer center after school without permission."

The computer center. So that's where they are going. Now Katie was more confused than ever. What were they up to?

Mandy and Suzanne might not have seen Katie, but Katie had heard what they were saying. And it made her really angry!

"Don't you feel bad about keeping a secret from Katie?" she heard Mandy ask Suzanne.

"After all, she's your best friend."

"She would just try to stop us," Suzanne said. "Katie's a goody-goody."

Katie scowled. This wasn't the first time Suzanne had said that. Katie was so angry, she wanted to scream. But she had to be quiet if she was going to find out what was going on.

Mandy continued down the hall. Suzanne followed close behind. When the girls finally reached the computer center, they stopped and looked around again.

Katie darted into a nearby bathroom to keep from being spotted. She stood there quietly, waiting until she heard the door to the computer center slam shut.

Katie slipped out of the bathroom, and headed toward the computer center. She stood outside the room and placed her ear against the wooden door. Unfortunately, she couldn't hear a thing.

Katie crouched down and tried to peek

into the room through the keyhole. But Katie couldn't see anything, either.

Just then, Katie heard footsteps in the empty hallway. She turned around just in time to see Mrs. Derkman, her third-grade teacher, walk up beside her.

"Katie, do you have an after-school activity today?" Mrs. Derkman asked.

Katie shook her head.

"Then what are you doing here?" Mrs. Derkman asked.

"I, um . . . well . . . I thought I dropped something," Katie told her nervously.

"You dropped what?" Mrs. Derkman demanded.

"I forget," Katie answered quickly.

"Well, *I'm* going to forget I saw you walking around in the hallway after the school day has ended—if you leave right now," Mrs. Derkman told her.

Katie knew Mrs. Derkman could get her into big trouble if she wanted to. "Yes,

ma'am," she answered. Then she turned and
raced down the hall and out of the school.

Chapter 7

There was no one outside the school building. By now, all the kids had gone home. Everyone except Mandy and Suzanne, that is. They were still in the computer room.

Katie wondered if Mrs. Derkman had found them in there yet. They were going to be in big trouble when she did.

Just then, Katie felt a cool breeze blowing on the back of her neck. She shivered slightly and lifted the collar of her jean jacket. But the breeze pushed right through it. No jean jacket could block out *this* wind. It was too strong.

This was the magic wind!

The magic wind picked up speed. It blew harder and harder, until it was circling right around Katie.

The magic wind became more powerful, whipping around Katie. She closed her eyes tight and tried not to cry.

Then it stopped. Just like that.

The magic wind was gone.

And so was Katie.

Slowly, Katie opened her eyes and looked around. The magic wind had blown her around to the back of the school building. Now she was standing outside, right near the window of the computer room. Through the window, Katie could see Mandy and Suzanne quietly sneaking out of the room.

Katie was still curious about what Suzanne and Mandy had been doing. But right now she had a bigger mystery to solve . . .

Who had the magic wind turned her into?

Katie looked down. She was wearing a pair

of black jeans, with big pockets and huge baggy legs. On her feet she was wearing black and orange sneakers with Velcro instead of laces.

Those were *George's* sneakers!

Quickly, Katie looked at the window. George's reflection stared back at her. That was one mystery solved. Katie was George. And she was going to be George until the magic wind came and switcherooed her back into Katie again.

Katie had no idea when that would be. So in the meantime, she might as well solve the *other* mystery: What were Suzanne and Mandy doing in the computer room?

Maybe they had left some sort of clue behind. Katie just *had* to get into the computer room . . . without bumping into anyone. That meant she couldn't be seen in the hallway. She would have to crawl through the window instead!

Katie opened the window wide enough for

her to move through. Then she remembered that George was a lot plumper than Katie was. She opened the window even wider.

Katie stuck her head in the room, and pulled the rest of George's body over the windowsill. She put her feet quietly on the ground, and walked over to the computers.

Unfortunately for Katie, Suzanne and Mandy had remembered to turn their computer off before they left the room. Now how was she supposed to know which one they had worked on?

Then Katie remembered something important. Computers got warm when they

were turned on. The one Mandy and Suzanne had just been using would have to be warmer than the others. Quickly, Katie moved around the room, touching each computer until she found one that was warm.

Katie switched the computer on and waited for it to boot up. Then she went straight to the history file. Her computer teacher, Mr. Beitman, had taught the fourth-graders that the history file had a list of all the most recently used documents.

The file opened. At the top of the list was a document called "4A Express."

Mandy had been working on the class newspaper, Katie thought to herself. *But why was Suzanne helping her? She isn't in class 4A. She is in class 4B.*

Katie double-clicked the file. Instantly, the front page of next week's *Class 4A Express* appeared on the screen.

Now Katie knew what Suzanne and Mandy had been up to. And it wasn't very nice at all.

Chapter 8

*MYSTERIOUS PRACTICAL JOKER
EXPOSED!*

Katie stared at the headline. Just beneath
it was a picture of George Brennan. Not just
any picture. Suzanne and Mandy had used
the worst picture of George they could find.
It was taken right after the pie-eating contest
at last year's school picnic. George had felt
really sick.

"That is so mean," Katie muttered to
herself.

There were other articles on the page, too.
They were the usual boring stories. One

headline read, "Mr. Kane Picks 4A to Lead Pledge of Allegiance." Another said, "4A Aces Math Tests." The headline next to that one read, "Art from Ink Stains."

But it was the big picture of George that stood out on the front page. There was no way anyone would miss that article.

And what a mean article it was:

Fake mice on the floor. Plastic throw-up in the salad bar. Whoopee cushions everywhere. Who has been responsible for these mean tricks? It's George Brennan, and now everyone knows it! George should be punished for causing so much trouble in the fourth grade. And so should anyone else who has been involved.

Katie gulped! When Mr. Guthrie read that, George could be in big trouble! So might Katie. After all, that whoopee cushion and the plastic throw-up had been hers.

Katie just couldn't let any of that happen. She was going to have to delete the article and get rid of that mean, awful picture of George.

Katie stared at the screen for a minute trying to figure out what to do. Mandy had been using a special program that was made to create newspapers. Katie had never used that program before.

I'll start by deleting the picture of George, Katie thought as she hit a few of the keys on the keyboard.

Bling! The alert sound rang out. The computer screen went blank.

Katie gulped. Had she just deleted all of Mandy's hard work? She hadn't meant to. She had only wanted to delete George's picture.

Bling! Just then, the alert sound rang out again. The front page of the newspaper flashed onto the screen.

Phew! Katie was so relieved.

But not for long. Katie had made a terrible

mistake. Sure, the picture of George was gone. But the picture of Mr. Kane had been made really big. So big, in fact, that all you could see was the principal's nose!

Katie had to fix that. She quickly double-clicked the mouse.

Bling! The screen went blank. Then the newspaper reappeared.

"Oh, no!" Katie cried out. Instead of fixing the front page, she'd made things worse. Part of the headline that had once read, "Mr. Kane Picks 4A to Lead Pledge of Allegiance," had been deleted.

Now, beneath the giant picture of the principal's nose it read: "Mr. Kane Picks."

Mr. Kane was definitely not going to like that. Katie had to fix it right away!

She began pressing more keys on the keyboard. *Bling!* The computer screen went blank. Then the front page of the newspaper reappeared.

This time, Katie realized she had changed

two headlines. "4A Aces Math Tests" and "Art from Ink Stains" had been mixed together. Now the headline read: "Math Test Stinks."

Oh, no! That wasn't what Mandy had written at all!

Katie began moving the mouse around the screen. She just had to fix this before someone found out what she had done.

Chapter 9

Bling! Bling!

The computer blurted out lots of warning sounds as Katie moved and clicked the mouse, trying to fix the newspaper. She moved her fingers as quickly as she could. But Katie wasn't fast enough.

Before she could make things right again, Mr. G. spotted her in the computer lab.

"George," the teacher called out as he walked into the room. "What are you doing?"

At first Katie didn't answer. She had been so focused on fixing the newspaper that she had forgotten that she was George now.

But Mr. G. had no idea that George was

really Katie. "George?" the teacher repeated.

"I . . . um . . ." Katie stammered.

Mr. G. didn't wait for her to think of an answer. Instead, he walked toward her, and peered over her shoulder at the computer screen.

"Oh, George," Mr. G. said. "This time you have gone too far."

"But Mr. G.," Katie began. "Mandy and Suzanne were going to print this awful picture of George . . . I mean of *me*, and—" Katie told the teacher.

Mr. G. shook his head. "That doesn't give you the right to make a mess of the *Class 4A Express*," he said.

Katie was shocked. Her teacher's voice was very stern—sort of like Mrs. Derkman's when she got angry. She had never seen Mr. G. like this before.

"But . . ." Katie began.

"No 'buts' about it, George," Mr. G. said. He took a deep breath. "You go on home now. We'll talk about this again in the morning."

There was no one outside the school building. Everyone was either at home or at an after-school activity. Katie was the only one there.

Suddenly, she felt a cool breeze blowing on the back of her neck. She pulled on the hood of George's black skateboarding sweatshirt. But she could still feel the cold wind.

Katie knew what that meant. This was no ordinary wind! This was the magic wind. No sweatshirt would ever block *that* out!

The magic wind swirled faster and faster. Before long, it was circling wildly around Katie, angrily blowing icy-cold wind right in her face.

And then it stopped. Just like that.

The magic wind was gone. Katie Carew was back.

And so was George Brennan. He was standing right next to Katie. Only *he* didn't know how he'd gotten there!

Chapter 10

"Katie Kazoo, what are you doing here?" George asked Katie. "Actually, what am *I* doing here? I don't remember coming back to the front of the school. All I remember is that I had skateboarding after school. Sort of." He frowned. "Boy, do I feel weird. For some strange reason I don't feel like I got to do any skateboarding at all."

Katie sighed. *Strange reason.* That pretty much said it all.

"So . . . uh . . . are you going home now?" she asked, trying to change the subject.

George nodded. "And then I'm going to the mall. I'm going to get a new pen."

"You're all excited about a pen?" Katie asked him. Now she was the one who was confused.

"Not just any pen. This pen has disappearing ink," George explained. "I thought I would loan it to someone. They'll use it to take notes. And in a few seconds, all their notes will disappear!" He began to laugh hysterically.

"That's not funny," Katie warned.

"Sure it is. You'll see," George assured her.

"Don't you think you're in enough trouble after this afternoon?" Katie said.

"What *about* this afternoon?" George asked her.

Katie frowned. Of course George didn't know what she was talking about. It was *Katie* who had been in the computer lab. Not George.

"So you don't remember anything about the computer room?" Katie asked him.

George scrunched up his face, thinking.

"Well, I *sort of* remember something about doing something with a computer. At least I think I do. I'm not sure. It's all kind of blurry. But I couldn't have been in there. I was at skateboarding. Wasn't I?"

Katie sighed. "I guess so. Sure," she said slowly.

But she knew that wasn't the truth. Still, she couldn't tell George about the magic wind. He never would have believed her.

But Katie had to make him believe her about one thing. The pranks had to stop. "Look, George, trust me," she warned. "No more practical jokes, okay?" George smiled, but didn't answer. Instead he hopped on his skateboard and rode off.

Chapter 11

"Sit down, everyone," Mr. Guthrie instructed the class as the bell rang.

Katie frowned. Usually, Mr. G. smiled when he said that. He was always anxious to get the day started. But today, her teacher was not grinning. He looked tired, and sort of sad.

Katie frowned. She knew why Mr. G. was upset. And she felt really badly about it. But probably not as bad as George was about to feel.

"Today we're going to learn a different kind of lesson," Mr. G. told the class.

The kids all sat there silently. They could tell something was very wrong.

"Yesterday, I found out that one of our students sneaked into the computer room after school," Mr. G. continued.

Katie looked over at George. He was sitting in his beanbag calmly. He really didn't know what Mr. G. was talking about.

Then Katie looked over at Mandy. Katie could tell she was kind of nervous by the way she was twirling her pencil. Mandy probably thought Mr. G. was talking about her and Suzanne.

"No one is allowed in the computer room without a teacher," Mr. G. continued. "You all know that."

"I was just working on the newspaper," Mandy blurted out. "I—"

Mr. G. looked at her with surprise. "You were in there, too?" he asked Mandy.

"Well, Suzanne and I were finishing an article, but—" Mandy began.

"Suzanne Lock was working on *our* class newspaper?" Mr. G. sounded confused. "Why would she do that?"

"She had information about the person who has been pulling all the practical jokes," Mandy said. "She was an unnamed source."

"Who you just named," Kevin Camilleri said. He laughed. "Nice one, Mandy."

Mandy blushed.

"Well, I have also discovered who our practical joker is," Mr. G. continued. "George, do you want to tell Mandy what you did to this week's *Class 4A Express*?"

"Me?" George replied. "I didn't touch the newspaper."

Mr. G. pulled a piece of paper out of his jacket pocket. "Are you saying you didn't do this?" he asked. He held up a copy of the front page of the newspaper.

Everyone stared at the paper.

Oh, boy, Katie thought nervously as she stared at Mr. Kane's giant nose, and the mixed-up headlines. *This is so not good.*

"I didn't do anything," George insisted. "At

least I don't *think* I did. I sort of remember being in the computer room, but I couldn't have been. I had skateboarding after school. At least I *think* I did."

"George," Mr. G. said sternly. "I saw you there."

"But, I didn't—" George began.

Before he could finish his sentence, Kevin began laughing. "George, that's hilarious!" he exclaimed. "Look at the size of Principal Kane's schnozzola!"

"Math tests definitely do stink," Kadeem chuckled. "This the funniest thing you've ever done, George."

Katie was surprised. Kadeem and George were always competing to be the funniest kid in the class. Having Kadeem give George that kind of a compliment was a huge deal.

George's face brightened. "It is pretty funny, isn't it?" he agreed. He puffed his chest out proudly. "I am *so* the King of Comedy!"

Before long, all the kids in the class were

laughing. Even Mandy. The only person who
wasn't laughing was Mr. G. He looked angry.
Very angry.

"I think these practical jokes have all gone
too far," the teacher said. "I have to take some
sort of action. So I am canceling the *Class 4A
Express.*" Everyone grew silent. They stared
at their teacher. He had never sounded like
this before.

The kids all knew better than to argue with their teacher. For the rest of the morning, they were very quiet. But when they got to the cafeteria, the kids in class 4A said *exactly* what they were thinking.

"It's not fair," Mandy insisted. "Why should we all be punished for what George did?"

"Yeah," Emma S. agreed. "We're going to be the only class in the school without a newspaper."

"Thanks a lot, George," Mandy continued. "You ruined everything."

Now George didn't look as proud as he had in class. He looked kind of upset.

That made Katie upset, too. After all, it hadn't *really* been George in the computer room yesterday.

"It isn't just George's fault," Katie pointed out to Mandy. "You were wrong, too."

"What did I do?" Mandy demanded.

"You wrote an article accusing George of being the practical joker when you had no proof. And you used that awful picture of him at the pie-eating contest," Katie accused her.

"How did you know about that?" Mandy said.

Oops.

"I didn't," Katie said quickly. "I was just trying to trick you into admitting it."

Phew. That was close.

"And you did!" Andrew shouted out. "Excellent, Katie!"

"She sure got you, Mandy," Kadeem added.

Some of the kids laughed.

Mandy blushed.

"It doesn't matter who did what," Emma Weber said with a sigh. "We still don't have a class newspaper anymore."

Katie sighed.

No one was laughing about that.

Chapter 12

Mandy stayed angry all day long. She was still complaining after school had ended. "I can't believe Mr. G. would do that to the newspaper!" she exclaimed as the kids in class 4A left the building that afternoon.

"It's your fault, Mandy," Kevin said. "Printing that picture and writing that article was mean to George."

Mandy stuck her nose up in the air. "I was just reporting a news story," she replied. "I thought people would find it interesting to know who the practical joker was."

"It would have been the only interesting story all year," Kevin told her.

"What's that supposed to mean?" Mandy demanded.

"He means the *4A Express* is boring!" Kadeem exclaimed.

Mandy's face turned all red. She looked like she was going to cry.

Now Katie felt doubly bad. First she had gotten George in trouble. Now the boys were upsetting Mandy.

"Yeah. At least what George wrote was funny," Andrew Epstein added.

" 'Mr. Kane Picks.' " Kevin laughed as he pretended to stick his finger up his nose. "That was classic!"

The boys began to laugh.

"Maybe we should have elected George to be the editor of the *4A Express*," Kevin continued. He put his arm around his best buddy's shoulders. "At least then we would have wanted to read it."

The boys were being too mean. Katie couldn't stand it anymore. "It's not like you were volunteering to write something for the newspaper. Mandy had to do it all by herself," she reminded them.

"That's true," Emma W. agreed. "We all could have pitched in to make it better."

But the boys didn't care what Katie and Emma W. thought.

" 'Math Test Stinks,' " Kadeem shouted out, remembering the headline. "I'll say. That test was really hard. It stunk like rotten skunk juice!"

The boys all started to laugh—except George. He just walked away.

Katie headed off after him. "What's wrong?" she asked.

"Nothing," George said. "I just feel kind of bad because we're the only class without a newspaper. Maybe I did go too far with my practical jokes. But I really don't remember messing up the newspaper."

Katie looked over at the crowd of laughing boys. They sure seemed to like the funnier version of the *Class 4A Express* a lot better than the serious one.

Suddenly, Katie got one of her great ideas.

"Maybe we don't need a class newspaper," she told him.

"Huh?" George asked.

"Can you stay at my house after cooking club on Saturday?" Katie continued.

"Sure, but what does that have to with . . ." George began.

"You'll see," Katie assured him with a grin.

Chapter 13

"Okay, you guys, don't forget to take your bags of fudge home with you," Mrs. Carew told the kids in the cooking club as they left Katie's house on Saturday afternoon.

One by one, the kids grabbed plastic bags filled with giant hunks of homemade chocolate fudge. Then they left to go home. Before long, only Mandy and George were left.

"I'll take my fudge later, Mrs. Carew," Mandy told Katie's mom. "Katie invited me over for a play date this afternoon."

"She couldn't have," George said. "Katie invited *me*."

George and Mandy both stared at Katie.

"I invited both of you," she told them.

"I'm not staying if *he's* going to be here," Mandy said.

"I'm not staying if *she's* going to be here," George said.

"You both have to stay," Katie told them. "I've got an idea about how we can make something even cooler than our class newspaper. But I need you guys to help."

"I'm not going to do anything George does," Mandy said.

"I'm not going to do anything Mandy does," George said.

"You *both* have to work on this. After all, you both had something to do with us losing the *4A Express*," she told them.

Mandy and George both opened their mouths to argue. But Katie wouldn't let them.

"I have a plan to fix things," she continued, before either of them had a chance to say a word. "But I need your help."

"What is your plan?" Mandy asked her.

"We should do a joke magazine," Katie said. "It could be filled with funny stories, goofy pictures, and even some silly headlines, like the ones I . . . I mean, *George* . . . made."

"A joke magazine *does* sound kind of cool," George admitted slowly.

"I think so, too," Katie agreed proudly. "But I'm not nearly as funny as you are."

"True," George boasted. "You do need me.

Count me in."

"Great," Katie said happily.

"But what do we need *her* for?" George asked, pointing to Mandy.

"Thanks a lot," Mandy grumbled.

"Be nice, George," Katie warned. "Mandy knows about the computer program that helps you lay out a newspaper. And she is also much better at grammar than we are."

"See, George," Mandy boasted. "Without me, you don't have a joke magazine." She turned to Katie. "We can download the newspaper program right into your computer," she explained.

"Great!" Katie exclaimed. "Let's get started."

Chapter 14

On Monday morning, Katie, George, and Mandy all got to school early. They wanted to make sure they were the first ones inside their classroom. That way, they could hand copies of their new magazine to each of their classmates as they walked into the room.

Katie, George, and Mandy were very proud of their work. They had spent all weekend working together at Katie's house making the magazine.

"*4A Funnies*," Emma W. said as she read the title.

"It's our new class joke magazine," George told her. "It's hilarious. I wrote a lot of it."

"It looks very nice, too," Mandy added. "*I* designed it."

A few moments later, Mr. G. walked into the room. "Sorry I'm late, dudes," he said. "I had a meeting with Mr. Kane."

The teacher looked around. All the kids were sitting on their beanbag chairs, reading *4A Funnies.*

"I thought we weren't going to have a newspaper anymore," Mr. G. reminded them.

"It's not a newspaper," Katie assured her teacher. "It's a joke magazine. George, Mandy, and I made it this weekend."

Mr. G. looked at Katie, George, and Mandy. "You guys did this all by yourselves?" he asked.

Katie nodded. "We used my computer."

"There are no mean jokes in this, are there?" Mr. G. asked.

Katie shook her head.

"Look at the pictures of George and Mandy making funny faces," Emma S. giggled. "George, you blew up your cheeks so big. You look like a balloon."

George smiled proudly.

"Mandy's touching her nose with her tongue," Kadeem pointed out as he stared at the photos. "Pretty impressive."

"This is hysterical!" Emma S. exclaimed. "Did you guys see the article on weird laws?"

"They're all real laws," George assured her.

"We found them in a book in the library," Katie added. She smiled at Mr. G. She knew he would like that. Teachers always liked it when you did research.

"Listen to this one," Andrew said. "In Massachusetts, it's against the law to put tomatoes in clam chowder."

"I could never live *there*!" Kevin exclaimed. "I love my tomatoes."

"In Kentucky, there's a law that says a person has to take a bath at least once a year!" Emma W. told the class.

"In the state of Colorado, if your cat goes outside loose it has to wear a tail light!"

Kadeem read. He turned to Katie. "I'll bet you're glad Cherrydale doesn't have a law like that for dogs!"

Everyone laughed as they pictured Katie's cocker spaniel with a light on his stubby little brown tail.

"This magazine is awesome," Kevin said. He looked over at Katie, George, and Mandy. "You guys totally rock!"

"Can we keep making *4A Funnies*, Mr. G.?" Katie asked hopefully.

Mr. G. smiled. "How can I say no when you dudes are all having so much fun reading?"

"All right!" Katie pumped her fist in the air.

"Woo-hoo!" George shouted. He gave Mandy a high five.

"Can I help with the next issue?" Andrew asked Katie.

"Me too," Kadeem added. "I could have my own column—'Kadeem's Craziest Jokes!'"

"There's already a 'George's Jokes' column," George told him. "It's on page three."

Kadeem turned the page and read some of George's riddles. "My jokes would be funnier than yours," he told George.

"I doubt it," George insisted.

"You can *both* have a joke column," Katie interrupted the boys before they could have an argument. "It will be like having a joke-off in every issue!"

"Maybe I could draw a comic strip," Emma

W. suggested shyly. "I like to draw."

"That would be really neat," Mandy said.

Katie grinned. It was good to see everyone getting along . . . *finally*.

"We are so lucky," Andrew said. "Everyone else just has a plain old class newspaper."

"It was time for a change," George said. "There haven't been any changes in this school for a long time."

Katie knew better. She thought about all the people she'd changed into in the past year—Mrs. Derkman, Emma W., Pepper, even George!

George was wrong. There *had* been plenty of changes in Cherrydale. But Katie was the only one who knew about them. And that was how it was going to stay!

Laughable Laws

Katie, George, and Mandy didn't have enough room to put all the silly laws they found in the library into the first issue of *4A Funnies*. But they didn't want you to miss out on all the fun. So, here are a few more of their favorites.

In Virginia, the law says that chickens cannot lay eggs before 8:00 a.m., and must be done before 4:00 p.m.

In Massachusetts, no gorilla is allowed in the backseat of any car.

An Alaska law says that you can't look at a moose from an airplane.

In North Dakota, it is illegal to lie down and fall asleep with your shoes and socks on.

You aren't allowed to drive a buffalo through a street in Kansas.

In North Carolina, it is against the law for dogs and cats to fight.

In Ohio, it is illegal to fish for whales on Sundays.

In Arkansas, it is against the law to mispronounce the name of the state. (Just in case you visit there someday, remember, it's pronounced AR-kan-saw!)